a min€dition book

published by Penguin Young Readers Group

Text and Illustrations copyright © 2007 by John A. Rowe

Original title: I Want a Hug

Coproduction with Michael Neugebauer Publishing Ltd., Hong Kong.

Rights arranged with "minedition" Rights and Licensing AG, Zurich, Switzerland.

Published simultaneously in Canada.

Manufactured in China by Wide World Ltd.

Typesetting in Cafeteria

Color separation by John Rowe.

Library of Congress Cataloging-in-Publication Data available upon request.

ISBN 978-0-698-40064-1

10 9 8 7 6 5 4 3 2 1

First Impression

For more information please visit our website: www.minedition.com

A big HUG for little Amy, J.A.R.

John A. Rowe

I want a Hug

minedition

At one end, Elvis the Hedgehog was as bristly as a scrubbing brush.

At the other, he was as prickly as a pine needle.

Little Elvis wanted nothing in the world as much as to be hugged.

So even when he asked nicely,

nobody would give him a hug.

"No, you're much too prickly!" they would say.

He saw lots of hugs in the town.
"Please, can I have one?" he asked.
"Shooo! Go away!" they'd say.
"You're much too prickly!"

He saw lots of hugs in the park.
"Can I have one too, just a little one?"
 he asked ever so nicely.
"Certainly not!" everyone answered.
"You're much too prickly!"

He saw lots of hugs at the soccer match.
"Can I please have one too?" he asked.
The players just laughed at him.
"Oh, please, please, please, I want a hug!" he cried.
But nobody would give him a hug because
of his prickles.

He saw lots of hugs at the train station.

"Could I please have a tiny hug?" he asked.

"Oooo no!" everyone cried, "not with those prickles!"

He saw lots of hugs at the hospital.

"Would you be so kind as to give me a hug too?"
he asked.

"What?!" all the patients shouted. "You're much too dangerous
with all those prickles...
Go away!"

Poor Elvis didn't know what to do any more...
he grabbed someone's leg...
"Oh please, won't you give me an itsy bitsy little hug?" he asked.
"No no no! Your prickles are much too prickly!"
the man answered. "Please let go of my leg!"

Elvis felt very sad, and he wondered if he would
ever find a hug.
Just then, he heard the strangest thing...
"Oh, won't anybody give me a kiss?
Just a little kiss is all I ask!"

It was Colin the Crocodile asking everybody for a kiss!
"Oooh no, you're much too ugly!" they said,
and nobody would give him a kiss.

"I'll give you a kiss!" called Elvis.
  Colin could hardly believe his ears!

"Oh, I could just hug you for that!" cried Colin
excitedly. He swept Elvis up in his arms and
gave him the biggest hug ever!

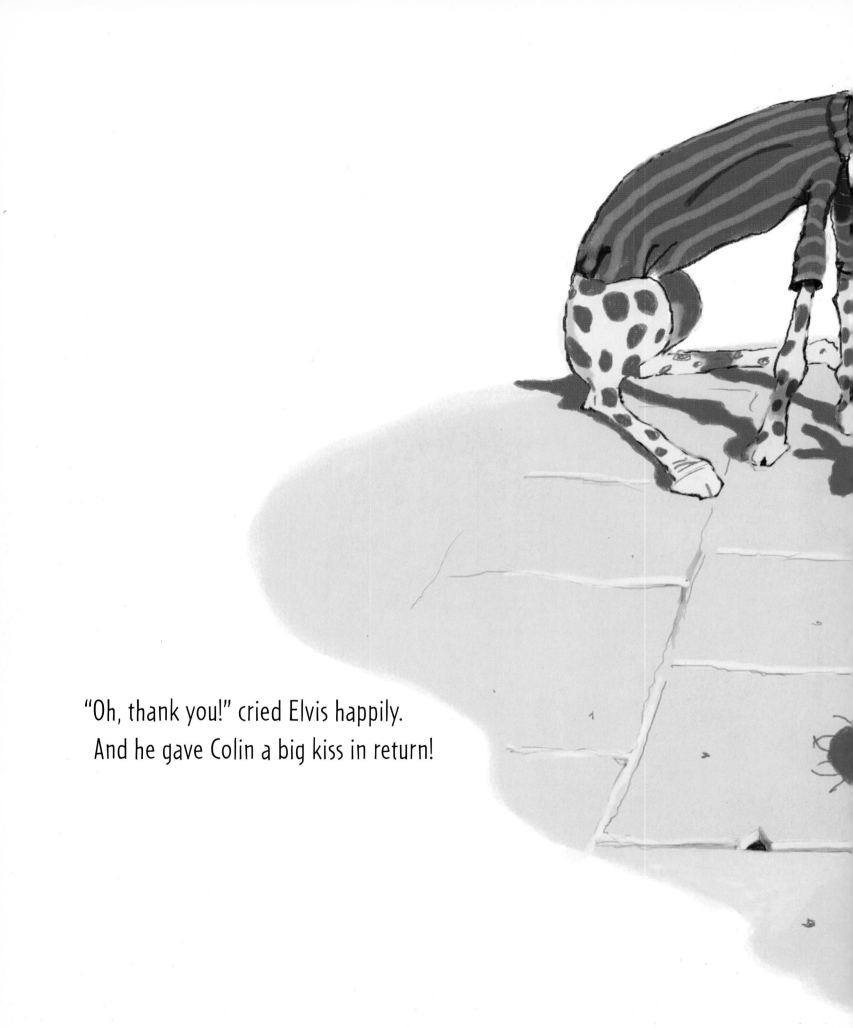

"Oh, thank you!" cried Elvis happily.
And he gave Colin a big kiss in return!

5-08